Curious George's 3-MINUTE STORIES®

Houghton Mifflin Harcourt
Boston New York

CONTENTS

MEET
Curious George ®
AND FRIENDS

This is George. He is a good little monkey and always very curious.

George lives with his friend the man with the yellow hat in an apartment in the city.

The doorman and Hundley are always there to greet them. Even if Hundley is just making sure George doesn't make a mess!

George has lots of city friends.
  He loves to visit Chef Pisghetti and his cat, Gnocchi, at
the restaurant. Chef Pisghetti makes the best spinach ravioli in
town! And his pizza? Perfecto!

When George goes to the museum, he always says hi to
Professor Wiseman.
      Sometimes, Professor Wiseman even needs special help from
George—like the time he went to outer space!

And George loves playing with his neighborhood friends Steve and
Betsy—and their dog, Charkie!

Sit, Charkie! Stay, Charkie! Now don't run away, Charkie!

Sometimes George and the man with the yellow hat visit their home in the country. They have great friends there too. Like their neighbor Bill and the farmers Mr. and Mrs. Renkins and their granddaughter, Allie.

Bill knows a lot about a lot, but he especially knows his way around a paper route. And Allie loves to explore, try new things, and dance—just like George!

But no matter where he goes or who he's with, George is always very curious about the world around him and ready for an adventure—just as long as he's back home in his own bed at the end of the day!

Curious George®

FINDS A FRIEND

Adaptation by Stephen Krensky
Based on the TV series teleplay
written by Bruce Akiyama

This is George. He was a good little monkey and always very curious. George had spent all day outside, exploring and listening to animal sounds.

Quack! Quack!

When George came home he was surprised to hear a strange sound in his house. CHIRP! CHIRP! He was not alone. But what was making the noise?

Could it be coming from the chair? George took a look.

Teddy!

Now the sound moved. CHIRP! It was not in the living room anymore. CHIRP! It seemed to be farther away. CHIRP!

It was in the bathroom. George looked all around for the sound. But he could not find it. He sat down to think.

A little duckie helped: SQUEAK! SQUEAK!

Soon the sound was coming from George's bedroom.

   CHIRP! It seemed to move from one place to another very quickly. CHIRP! George tried to follow it.

   He did not find anything . . . except a mess!

George's friend the man with the yellow hat was outside. He heard the chirping too.

"That's a cricket," he explained. "He probably wants to get out of our house. Crickets like the light. If you make everything dark, maybe you can get his attention with a flashlight. Once you catch him, you can help him go home."

George decided to try. He shut off all the lights and got ready. At the first CHIRP! CHIRP! he sprang into action.

He flipped the switch on his flashlight . . . and caught a cricket!

Then George brought the cricket to the back porch. He opened the bag to let the cricket out. But the cricket did not leave.

Where did he go?

He was already home.

Curious George®

CIRCUS ACT

Adaptation by Rotem Moscovich
Based on the TV series teleplay
written by Grant Moran

This is George. He loves to help out at his friend Chef Pisghetti's Italian restaurant. Today Chef had a very special order.

It was a large order, and George was excited to help cook and be the delivery monkey.

Is that a circus tent? Yes!
George was delivering to the
Flying Zucchinis, the amazing
acrobat troupe.

He loved to watch
them practice. Leo Zucchini
showed off, balancing the
pizza box on a long stick.

Then Gnocchi the cat
arrived. Oh no! Cats made
Leo sneeze . . .

ACHOO! Gnocchi,
please don't get too close!

Up above, Clare Zucchini was balancing on the high wire.

George wanted to try too. But the mop was not a good balancing pole. "Move your hand closer to the heavy end!" Clare said. Phew! That was much better.

That night was the Zucchinis' first big tent show. The audience oohed and aahed. Suddenly Gnocchi the cat walked out onto the high wire and Leo started to sniffle and lose his balance. Uh-oh, don't sneeze!

George came to the rescue. Gnocchi turned away from the acrobats and jumped onto George's balancing pole.

George moved his hand closer to the heavy side of the pole to keep his balance, just as he had done with the mop. The show was saved!

Afterward, the acrobats made George an official Zucchini. Clare told the man with the yellow hat and their friend the chef that George was a natural.

Whoops . . . But maybe George should stick to the high wire!

Curious George®

GOES BOWLING

Adaptation by Cynthia Platt
Based on the TV series teleplay
written by Raye Lankford

Friday night was bowling night. For George and the man with the yellow hat, this Friday was extra special. It was the night of the bowling championship.

    Mr. and Mrs. Renkins and the Quints were bowling against the man, but who would win?

After the game, Mr. Renkins announced, "It's a tie! That means there will be a tiebreaker tomorrow night." George was so excited.

"Want to use my practice ball to roll one, George? I never let anyone use my lucky yellow ball. It's the only one I ever hit a strike with!" said the man.

George rolled . . . but the ball went into the gutter. Oh no, a gutter ball!

George always seemed to roll them.

The next morning, George decided he wanted to help out—and
polish the man's lucky yellow bowling ball for him!
　　　George lifted the ball out of the bag and gave it a test roll.
It rolled really well . . .
　　　But then it kept on rolling—

Yuck! If that ball didn't need polishing before,
it definitely needed it now.

George worked hard. That kind of cleaning takes
real monkey elbow grease.

Then the clean ball needed a test drive. George rolled it on the smooth, hilly driveway.
But it was a little too smooth and hilly.

George grabbed his wagon and rushed to save the ball!

Later that evening, the man rushed to get his bowling bag and shoes. "George," said the man, "are you ready? We're running late."

They were just about to drive to Bowlmor Lanes when George realized that the man had taken the wrong bag. His lucky ball was in the other bag.

George jumped out of the car and ran to get the ball . . . and returned to find that the man, thinking George was still in the car, was already gone!

George climbed a tree to think. The man needed his lucky bowling ball. But how could George get it to him?

He had an idea. From the tree, the road to Bowlmor Lanes looked a little like a big bowling lane with gutters.

And if there was one thing George was good at, it was rolling gutter balls!

With George's help, the man's lucky yellow bowling ball rolled uphill and down.

Finally, it rolled right into the parking lot of Bowlmor Lanes and then through the front door and right toward the bowling lanes!

The ball rolled past the man with the yellow hat and down the lane—

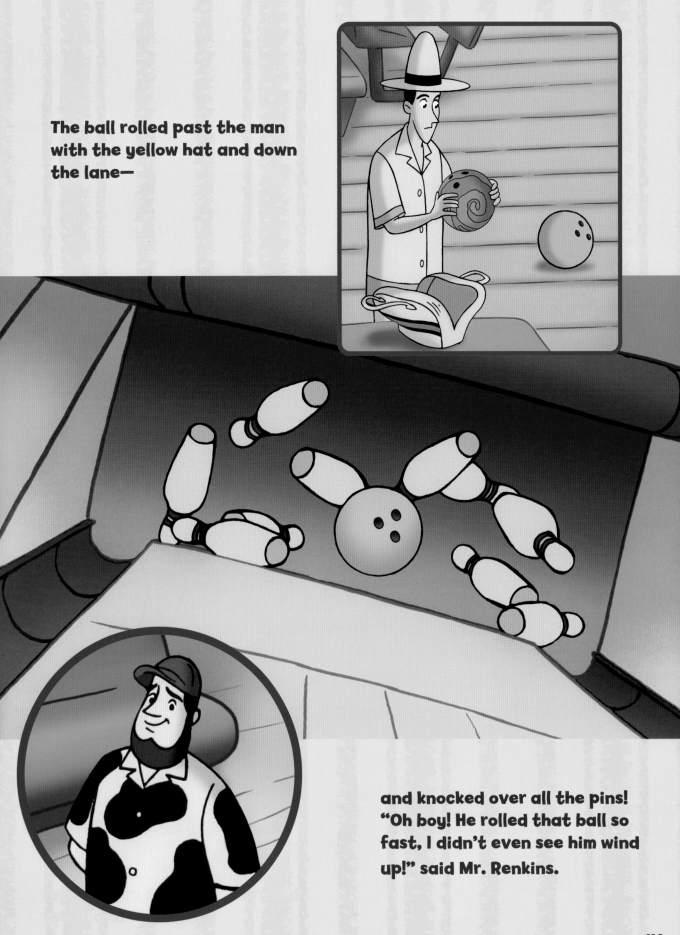

and knocked over all the pins! "Oh boy! He rolled that ball so fast, I didn't even see him wind up!" said Mr. Renkins.

Everyone celebrated, especially George. It was his best roll ever!

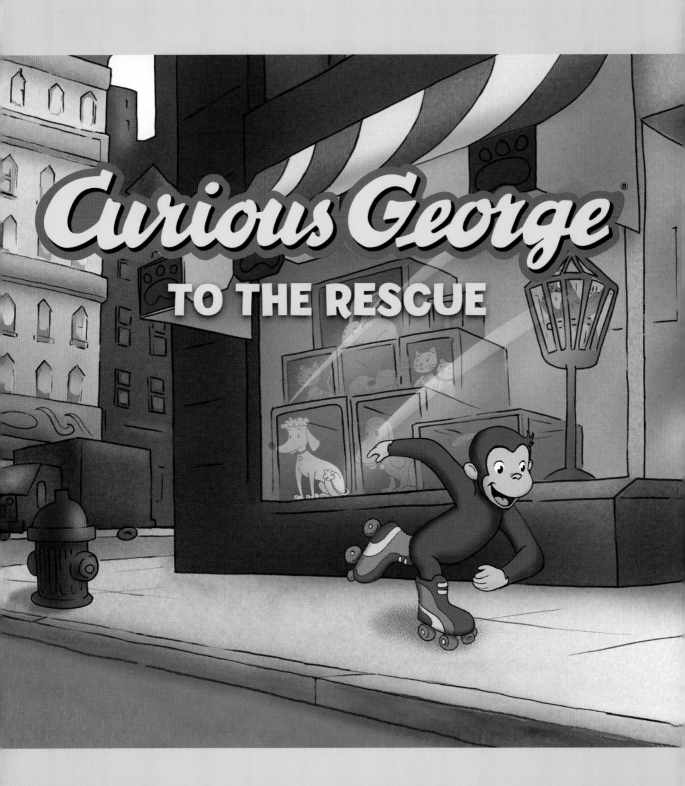

Curious George

TO THE RESCUE

Based on the TV series teleplay
written by Lazar Saric

This is George. He was a good little monkey and always very curious. Today George was curious about roller-skating! Hundley the dachshund was the first to try out the new skates.

Hundley went fast!

Too fast!

George followed his runaway
roller-skating friend.
Red light means stop.

Green light means go!

Hundley hoped the girls in the
park would help him stop.
        But they just sent him on
his way again . . . backwards!

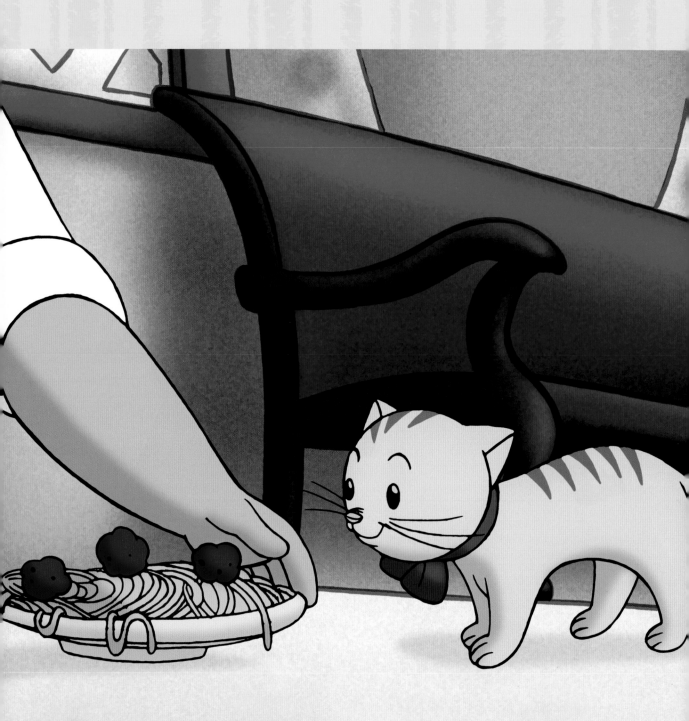

Would George catch up with Hundley in front of the spaghetti shop?

Look out! Gnocchi the cat is in Hundley's path.

And look out, George!

George caught up to Hundley and Gnocchi at the top of the steepest hill in the city. He was just in time . . . to join them on a wild ride into the lake!

George walked his friends
home. They were wet and
muddy. George thought
they'd had a good
adventure.

Hundley, however,
didn't plan to go skating
again—anytime soon.

Curious George®

TIME FOR SCHOOL

Adaptation by Cynthia Platt
Based on the TV series teleplay
written by Kathy Waugh

Today is a great day to be a curious monkey! George is going to kindergarten with his friend Allie. At 7:00, he starts to get ready. "Don't forget an apple for the teacher," says the man with the yellow hat.

George makes sure he has his school supplies. There will be so many things to learn and do at school.

At 8:00, George and Allie are at the bus stop, waiting patiently. The bus arrives right on time, and they hop on and ride to school.

George and Allie arrive at school at 9:00.

George is very happy to meet Allie's classmates.

The teacher calls everyone together at 10:00 for story time.
The students all sit in special chairs to listen to the teacher read.
    Then the students talk about what they like most about the
story. George likes the part about castles.

What fabulous fun! At 11:00, it's time to play at the water and sand tables.

George loves to play with sand—and to make a mess. Maybe it's cleanup time too!

At 12:00, it's time to eat lunch! George and Allie are feeling hungry after so much playing and learning.
They sit down and enjoy their lunches from home.

Wow—the day is flying by! At 1:00, George and Allie are playing with blocks. He wonders if they could use them to build a castle in the classroom. But George gets a little carried away . . .

Luckily, the teacher loves the fancy castle they built for her.

It's 2:00—time to go home!
George has had such a
wonderful day at school.

Curious George®
DANCE PARTY

Adaptation by Borana Greku & Alessandra Preziosi
Based on the TV series teleplay
written by Raye Lankford

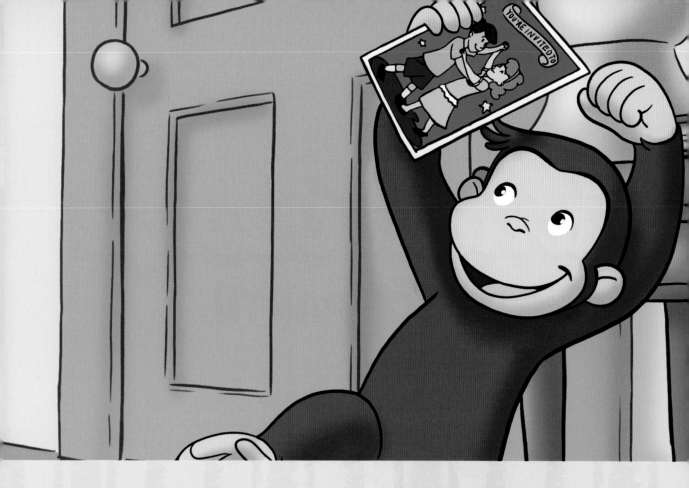

George was excited. He had just received an invitation to Allie's dance party! He couldn't stop dancing! He danced while he brushed his teeth.

Sometimes he even danced while he slept.

But George's friend Bill didn't want to go to the party. "I'll be the only kid who can't dance," Bill said.

"Look," said Bill, "even Mr. and Mrs. Renkins are practicing for the party!"

"This is called the box step," said Mrs. Renkins. George was curious. He didn't know that dance.
     The dance looked hard. Bill didn't think he could learn it. "Maybe I should tell Allie I have the chickenpox!" he said.

"Dancing should have a map. Maps show you where to go," Bill said.

George thought that was a great idea! He counted the dance steps and made a map. Right steps were red and left steps were blue. He numbered them and made the quick steps smaller than the slow steps.

When they got home with their
map, something was still missing.
     George thought about Mr.
and Mrs. Renkins. Of course! They
needed music!

The beat of the music made dancing much easier. He just moved his feet to the rhythm.

The night of the party arrived. Bill was still worried. "I'll look silly using the map," he said.

George looked at the map again. The steps were shaped like a box! All they had to do was make a box with their feet.

Bill danced with Mrs. Renkins. "You dance beautifully!" she exclaimed.

"I wish I could do that dance," Allie said. Bill and George were surprised. "You mean you don't know it?" Bill asked.

"I don't know any fancy dances," Allie said. "I just move to the music!"

Bill had been worried about dancing for no reason!
"Could you teach that dance to the rest of us?" Allie asked.

Allie turned on the music. She and George were dance partners.

Bill took out the map. He showed everyone how to do the box step.

George and Bill danced all evening. It was great teaching everyone the box step, but it was even more fun dancing with friends.

Curious George®

LEMONADE STAND

Adaptation by Erica Zappy Wainer
Based on the TV series teleplay
written by Gentry Menzel

George loved playing soccer. But he needed a new ball.

"When I was young, I got a new soccer ball by running a lemonade stand," the man with the yellow hat said.

The man with the yellow hat was going out. "I have to go out for a bit now. Speaking of lemonade, we can have some together when I get home, George!" the man said.

George looked at the lemonade in the refrigerator. This gave him an idea. He really wanted a new soccer ball.

George brought the lemonade downstairs. He set up his lemonade
stand outside his apartment building and waited.

Out came the doorman. He was hot. "Hey, is that lemonade?" he asked. George handed him a full carton of lemonade.

"That's too much, George! Do you have any cups?" the doorman asked. George ran inside. He came back with cups and filled one up to the top.

"I still can't drink all of that, George!" the doorman said.

The doorman poured half the lemonade into another cup. "That's better," he said. George didn't know you could make one cup of lemonade into two cups.

The doorman gave George a quarter for the lemonade. A quarter? George was confused. Where was the soccer ball?

Soon George saw Betsy. "I can help you sell lemonade," Betsy said.

Sell? Now George understood. He needed to earn the money to buy a soccer ball.

Betsy had seen a construction site nearby. The workers were tired and thirsty. It would be a great spot to sell lemonade.

It didn't take long for the workers to line up! Everyone loved George's lemonade. His stand was a success.

Soon George was down to his last two cups of lemonade. But there were still four thirsty workers in line! George remembered the doorman's trick. He split the two cups in half to make four.

Now George had enough money to buy a soccer ball. George and Betsy went straight to the toy store to buy one.

Then George remembered his friend. The man was looking forward to a glass of lemonade, but George had sold it all. George had one more big idea.

George used his money to buy more lemonade. But his friend had a big idea too! He brought home a new soccer ball for George. George was a very happy monkey.

Curious George®

CHASES THE RAINBOW

Adaptation by Amy E. Cherrix
Based on the TV series teleplay
written by Michael Maurer

It was a beautiful day in the country. Steve, Betsy, and their dog, Charkie, were visiting from the city for the first time. George couldn't wait for their outdoor adventure to begin. But first they had to unpack.

When Betsy dropped her books, George saw something amazing. "That's a rainbow, George!" said Betsy. "See the pot of gold at the end? And the leprechaun? Rainbows are always the same seven colors: red, orange, yellow, green, blue, indigo, and violet."

While Betsy told George about rainbows, the man helped Steve prepare for a hike.

"Have you ever seen any wild animals?" Steve asked.

"We've got skunks and deer. I've even seen a moose or two," the man replied.

"A moose!" Steve said. "Now, there's something you don't see in the city."

At last it was time for their hike. "I'm driving into town to get food for dinner," said the man. Just then thunder grumbled low in the distance. "If it rains, head home," he added. "George knows the way."

George led them into the forest. "I'm not leaving without a picture of a moose," Steve said. Just then he felt a raindrop. "Oh no. Not rain! Do we have to go back already?"

"I don't think so," Betsy said. "It's probably going to stop soon. Look! The sun is already peeking through the clouds."

When George turned around, there was a huge colorful rainbow arcing across the sky!

"That's the biggest rainbow I've ever seen," said Betsy.

George was excited to have found a rainbow. But he couldn't see the pot of gold from here.

"I'm climbing this tree to take a picture," Steve said. George
needed a better view too. He knew if he was going to find the pot
of gold, he needed to get closer. George ran off in search of the
rainbow's end with Charkie close behind.

"Charkie! George! Wait!" Betsy yelled, chasing them through
the rain.

When Betsy finally caught up with them, George tried to explain that he had wanted to reach the pot of gold. But no matter how far or fast he and Charkie ran, the rainbow only got farther away.

"The leprechaun with a pot of gold is just a fairy tale," said
Betsy. "But I guess it couldn't hurt to look just in case."
    They hadn't gone far when something small and green
hopped through the bushes. Could it be the leprechaun? George
thought he must be getting close to the pot of gold now.

But it was only a green frog. Usually George would be happy to meet a frog, but it was no leprechaun.

George wasn't disappointed for long, though, because the frog had led him to a second rainbow!

"Sorry, George," Betsy said. "That's not another rainbow—it's only the reflection of the rainbow on water."

Meanwhile, Steve realized he was lost. Suddenly something moved in the bushes.

"A moose!" Steve shouted, snapping a picture. But the moose didn't like Steve's loud voice, or his camera.

"Back away from the moose slowly," a boy said. It was George's friend Bill. He knew a lot about the wilderness. "And whatever you do, don't frighten it," Bill added.

The moose walked off into the forest.

    When the coast was clear, Bill introduced himself.

    "Can you help me find my sister and our friend George?" Steve asked.

    "I know George," Bill said. "Follow me. I saw his friend in town. He'll help us."

"Steve!" said the man. "Where are Betsy, Charkie, and George?"

"We got separated in the woods," Steve said. "George saw a rainbow and they ran off."

"If I know George, I bet he went to find the gold at the end of the rainbow. I have an idea to help him get home," the man said.

George and Betsy were trying to find their way home.
     Suddenly, Charkie began to bark. Something was glowing
from the end of the rainbow! It must be their pot of gold! They
raced toward the light.

"George! Over here," called the man with the yellow . . . balloon! He was standing on the roof of their house, holding a bright, shiny balloon that was wearing a very familiar yellow hat.

George was happy to be home with his friends. There was no pot of gold, but he knew he had found the real treasure at the end of the rainbow.

Curious George

CATCHES A COLD

Adaptation by Erica Zappy
Based on the TV series teleplay
written by Peter Hirsch

George's favorite day of the week was Sauce Day at Chef Pisghetti's restaurant. He always gave Chef Pisghetti some tips to make the best sauce. But today, instead of being able to taste the chef's new Molto Jolto sauce, George couldn't taste anything!

Chef Pisghetti sent George home, and the man with the yellow hat sent George to bed. Then he took George's temperature.
"Fever. Stuffy nose. Clammy paws," said the man. "You are definitely fighting a germ, George."

The man got out a book. There was a picture of a funny-looking blob. "There are good germs and bad germs. A bad germ is making you sick, George," the man explained.

"Germs are very small. They can be found anywhere in your body: your nose, your mouth, your stomach, your lungs. But that's enough biology for today. Tired monkeys need their rest."

George might have been sick, but he was still curious. Where did the germ come from? And more important, how could he get rid of it? He was still wondering when he dozed off . . .

Soon George was dreaming. In his dream he was very small . . . like a germ! He and his pal Gnocchi were going to take a trip inside George's sleeping body to fight off the bad germs.

George and Gnocchi zoomed into sleeping George's mouth and landed right on his tongue. It was soft and squishy. And there was music playing! They hadn't expected that! What could it be? It seemed to be coming from his nose.

When George and Gnocchi got to the nose, they saw a funny-looking blob strumming a guitar and singing!

"I'll make you sniff and I'll make you sneeze,
You won't be smelling that smelly cheese!
We'll be making you sweat and making you squirm,
Because that's how germs are being germs!"

George could hardly believe his eyes.

"I'm Toots, the singing germ," he introduced himself, "and these are my backup singers, the Germettes."

Seeing Toots in his nose made George upset. He wanted that germ out of him!

But Toots did not want to go. In fact, he took the Germettes and headed to George's lungs, laughing and singing all the way.

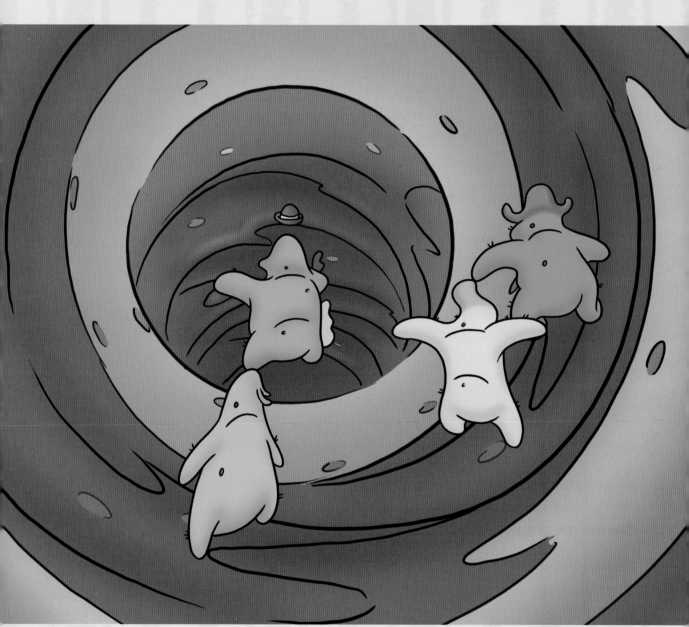

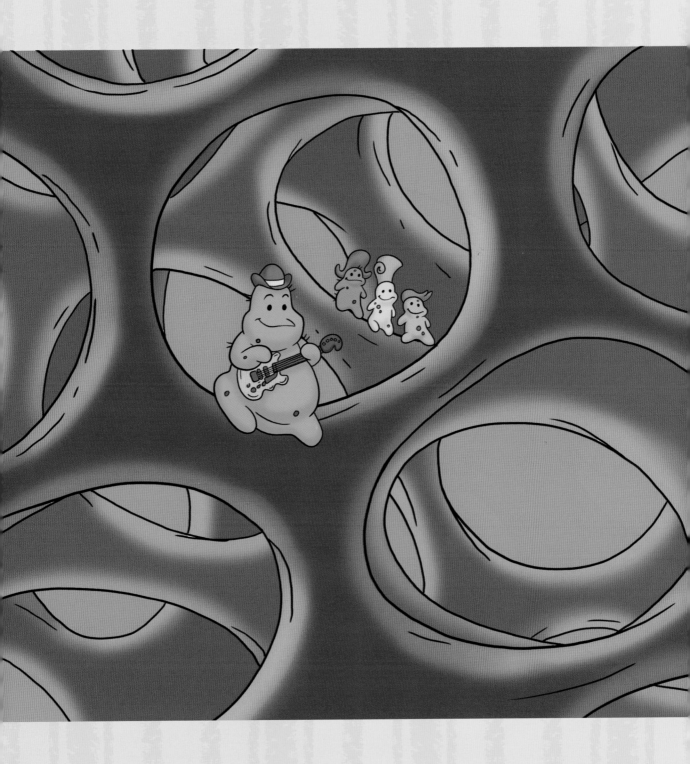

George and Gnocchi chased the germs to the lungs. George noticed that when the lungs got smaller, air went out. And when the lungs got bigger, a rush of air came in. He was watching himself breathe!

George's lungs gave him an idea. He remembered something he saw in the germ book: coughing and sneezing are the lungs' way of doing their job and trying to force out bad germs.

All George had to do was sneeze Toots right out of his body!

George and Gnocchi chased Toots and the Germettes all the way to George's nose.
    Then, with some well-positioned tickling, George sent Toots and the Germettes flying out of his nose with one big sneeze!

When George woke up from his dream, he went straight to the bathroom to wash his hands—and feet—just in case. After the icky adventure with Toots, this little monkey wanted to keep germs far away!

A few days later, George was feeling much better. He had taken lots of naps, drunk lots of water and juice, and sneezed out those germs. He could even smell again!

Curious George
BLASTS OFF

Adaptation by Monica Perez
Based on the TV series teleplay
written by Craig Miller & Joe Fallon

Professor Wiseman invited George and his friend the man with the yellow hat to visit her at the space center. Professor Einstein and Professor Pizza needed help, and she thought they might be able to lend a hand.

"How can we help?" asked the man.

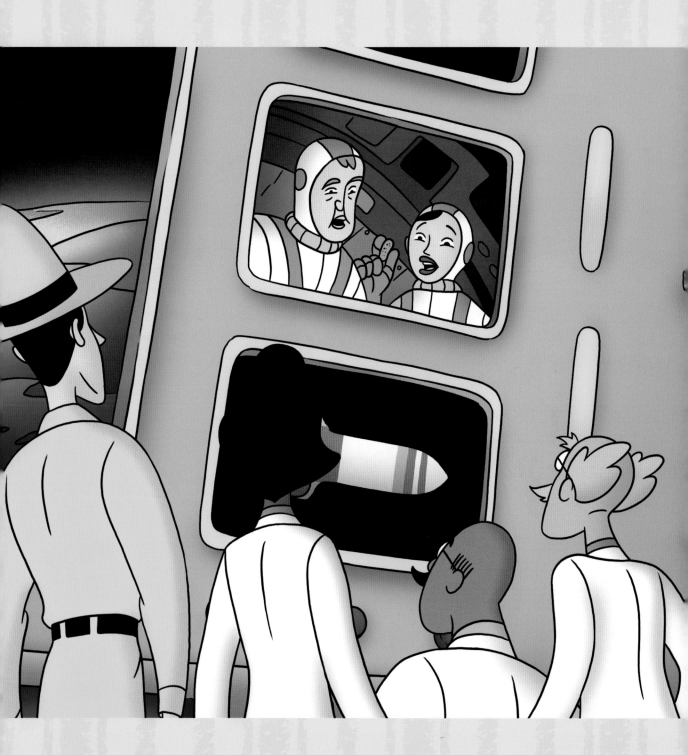

The scientists began to brief the man on his mission: to restock the space station's food supply. The astronauts on the station had discovered they had only one peanut left to eat.

The man with the yellow hat was planning to ride a space shuttle up through Earth's atmosphere into space. He would enter orbit around Earth and pass near the space station in order to make his delivery.

Of course, George was disappointed he wouldn't be able to come along.

But in order for the man to release the supplies, he needed to be able to push four buttons at the same time. The man only had two hands. He couldn't do that, but a monkey could. George was thrilled to help!

The hungry scientists on the space station would soon have more than one peanut to eat. George would also deliver some new supplies to help them with science experiments.

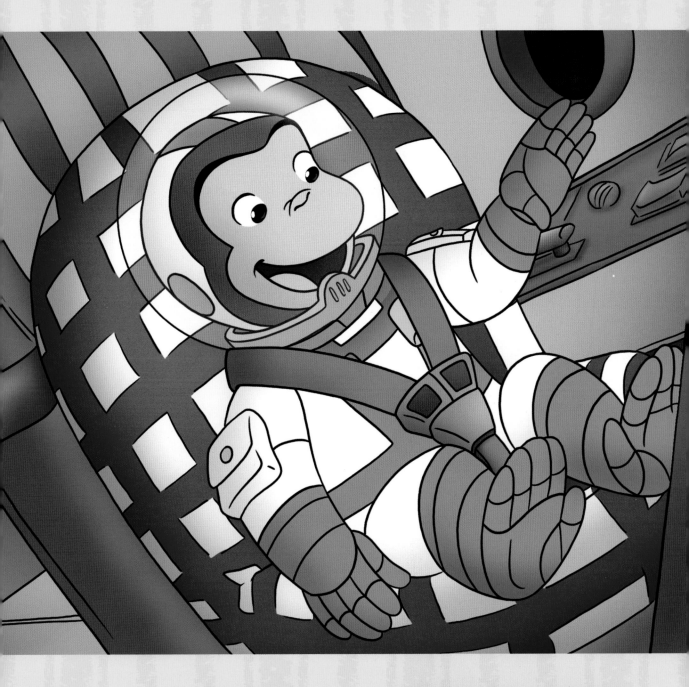

"You must launch the payload at
exactly the right moment,"
Professor Einstein said to George.
George nodded. He would have to
listen to instructions carefully.

Liftoff was a success, but then George wanted to look at the supplies. He took them out to play, but he couldn't get them back inside quickly enough. George missed the payload launch! He passed right by the space station without sending the supplies.

George would have to orbit Earth one more time!

"George, you have enough fuel for only one more orbit. You have to get the supplies back in their containers. The next time you pass the station will be the last chance. Then we have to bring you home," warned Professor Wiseman.

George was used to cleaning his room. It was good practice for cleaning up the mess in the spaceship.

He was ready in time to launch the supplies.
    Hooray! They made it to the space station!

George had one more task to complete. He had to make it back to the ground safely! To do this the shuttle had to reenter Earth's atmosphere at the right moment.

It was a good thing George listened to instructions this time. He pulled the lever that controlled the ship's direction. He could now land the ship back at the space center. His friends congratulated him on a successful mission!

George had a blast going to outer space. He couldn't wait to do it again.

Curious George®

SAYS GOOD NIGHT

Written by Karen Pandell

Good night, George.
It's been a day
of curious things
and games to play.
With all your friends,
you've had your fun.
Now night is falling.
Day is done.

You know what to do,
little sleepyhead.
You're a tired little monkey,
and it's time for bed.

Are you sleepy yet?

138

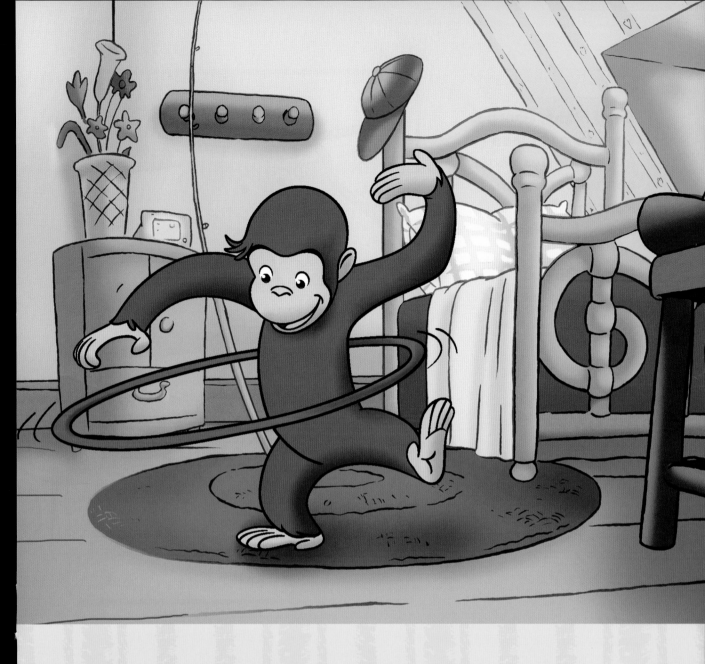

Good night, George.
Open the door.
Time to pick up the toys on the floor.
Instead you stop to play with blocks.
Don't forget to watch the clock!

Are you sleepy yet?

Good night, George.
Time to get clean
in the sudsiest bath
you've ever seen.
Pour in the soap
so the bubbles will grow.

Oh my! Oh no!
Watch it overflow!

Brush your teeth.
See them shine.
Head for bed.
You look so fine.

Are you sleepy yet?

Good night, George. Time for a look at your favorite bedtime storybook.

George and Jumpy sailed so high. Holding a kite, they crossed the sky.

George's friend came right away. He took them home and saved the day.

Are you sleepy yet?

Good night, George.
Time for a kiss
and the bedtime game you never miss.
Under the hat, cover your face . . .
aren't you fond of your hiding place?
One last round of peek-a-boo!
Now lift the hat, and I see you!
(Okay, George—another round or two.)

Are you sleepy yet?

A LULLABY FOR GEORGE

Good night, George.
Hush, hush. The world gets ready for bed.
A cooing pigeon tucks his head.
A tiger-stripe kitten curls up in a ball
with a little dachshund asleep in the hall.
A bushy-tailed squirrel is snug in his tree.

Here is a lullaby
for you from me . . .
Hush, hush.
Little monkeys
must close their eyes
so they grow up to be
curious and wise.

Are you sleepy yet?

Good night, George.
Settle into bed.
Time to rest that curious head.
Close your eyes good and tight.
What stories will shine in your dreams tonight?
Rest for the morning, a day bright and new . . .
when a curious mind will find lots to do!

Shhh . . . George is sleeping.